Print information available on the last page

Rev. date: 07/27/2015

. To order additional copies of this book, contact:
Xlibris
1-888-795-4274
www.Xlibris.com
Orders@Xlibris.com

Rosie the Witch

William Bix

Illustrations by Mark Ruben Abacajan

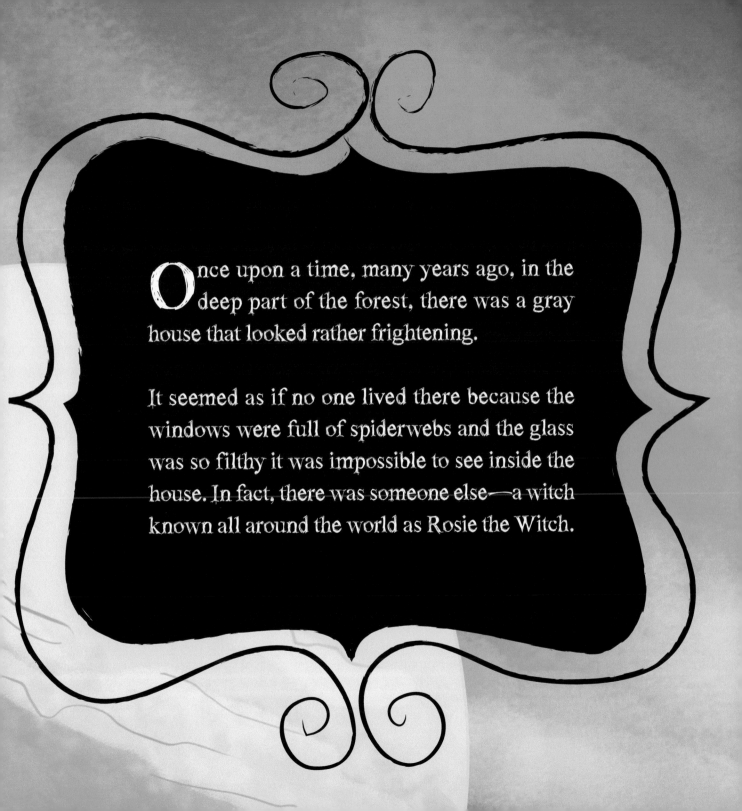

Once upon a time, many years ago, in the deep part of the forest, there was a gray house that looked rather frightening.

It seemed as if no one lived there because the windows were full of spiderwebs and the glass was so filthy it was impossible to see inside the house. In fact, there was someone else—a witch known all around the world as Rosie the Witch.

Rosie the Witch had a wart right on top of her bumpy, crooked nose. She had big dark eyes and crazy black-and-white hair. She was a very ugly witch and was scary to look at.

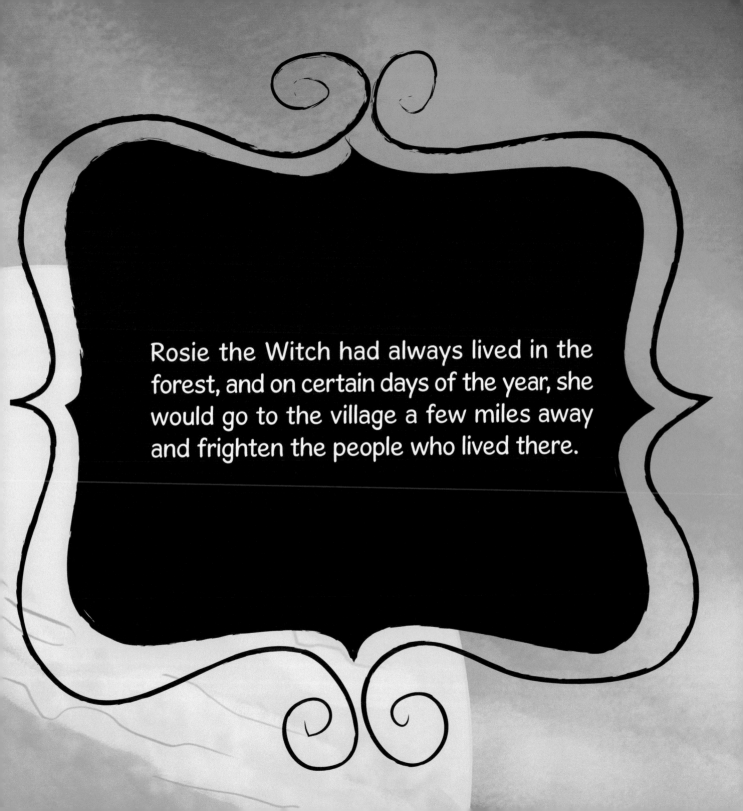

Rosie the Witch had always lived in the forest, and on certain days of the year, she would go to the village a few miles away and frighten the people who lived there.

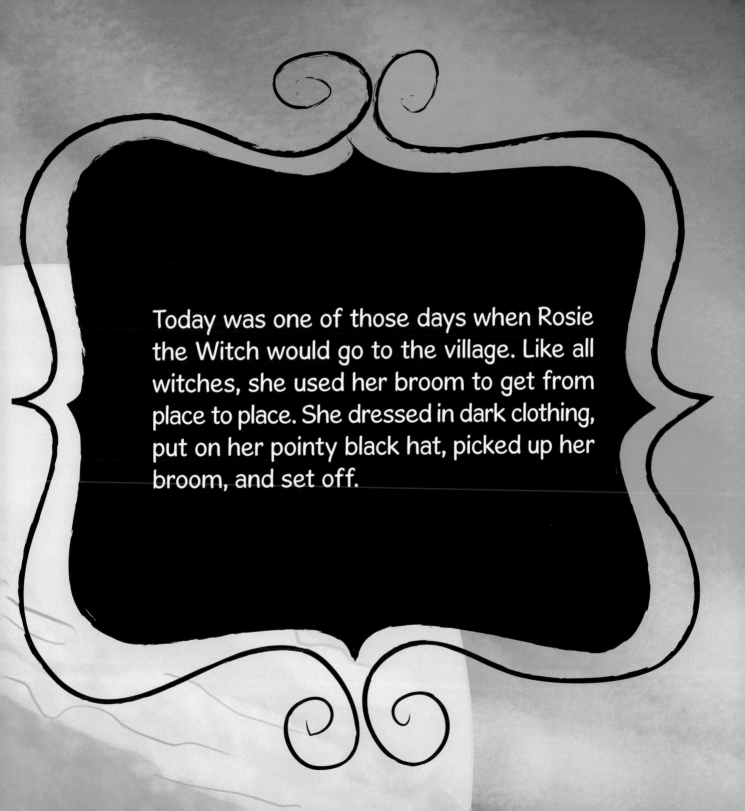

Today was one of those days when Rosie the Witch would go to the village. Like all witches, she used her broom to get from place to place. She dressed in dark clothing, put on her pointy black hat, picked up her broom, and set off.

As the sun set, Rosie the Witch arrived at the village.

When some of the villagers out on the street saw the silhouette flying on her broom, they went running to their houses as fast as a blink of an eye. Rosie the Witch couldn't stop cackling to see the people flee in fear.

Suddenly, a little voice from the street called to the witch. "Are you Rosie the Witch?" The witch halted on her flying broom, stared at the girl, and wondered why she hadn't run away like everyone else did.

"Yes, I am Rosie the Witch." Libby, the little girl, asked, "Why do you come to the village to frighten people?" The witch was puzzled. After a little while thinking about it, she eventually replied, "I am going to tell you a secret, little girl. You can see for yourself that we witches are ugly. We have warts on our noses and we fly on broomsticks, and the only thing we do when we come to the village is to buy food. When people see us, we get scared."

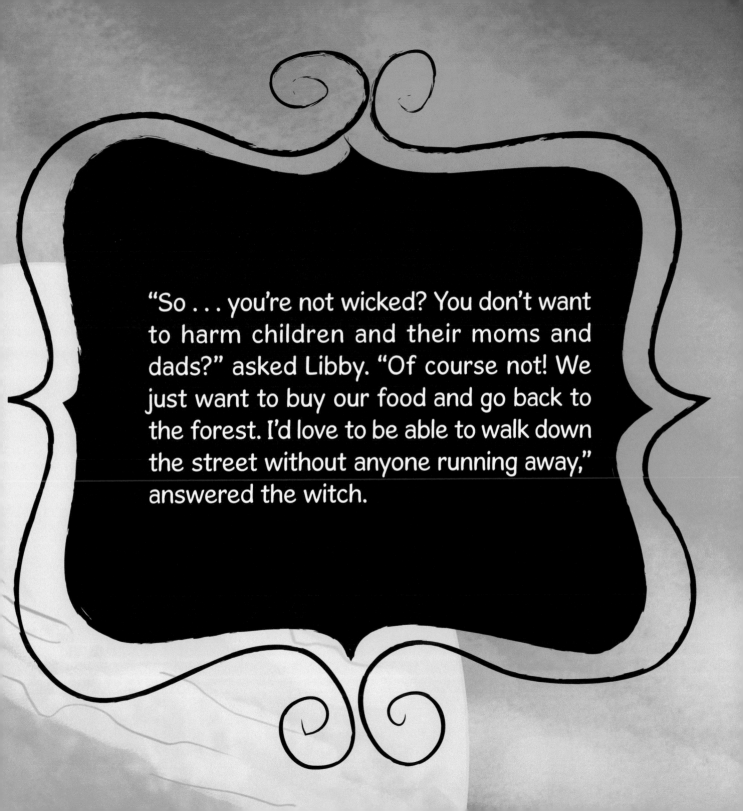

"So . . . you're not wicked? You don't want to harm children and their moms and dads?" asked Libby. "Of course not! We just want to buy our food and go back to the forest. I'd love to be able to walk down the street without anyone running away," answered the witch.

So Libby decided to go home to get her brother, Anthony, and her two cousins, Lucy and Felicity, to help spread the word to the whole village the true story. They went house to house, telling people that witches were good and would not hurt even a fly.

And that was how it came about that witches began to live alongside the villagers without scaring them, and the villagers learned to value a person's character and not their appearance because sometimes looks can be deceiving.

Printed in the United States
By Bookmasters